DISNEY's

THE LITTLE MERMAID

THE BOYFRIEND MIX-UP

Disney's

THE LITTLE MERMAID

THE BOYFRIEND MIX-UP

by Katherine Applegate

Disney PRESS

NEW YORK

Look for all the books in this series:

Drawings by Philo Barnhart
Cover painting by Fred Marvin
Inking by Russell Spina, Jr.

Library of Congress Catalog Card Number: 93-72888

ISBN: 1-56282-642-5

FIRST EDITION

1   3   5   7   9   10   8   6   4   2

This book is for Kelsey

To aunt Jane
and Pauline
July '94

Ox love always,
Russell Jr.

Disney's

THE LITTLE MERMAID

THE BOYFRIEND MIX-UP

"Doesn't this place look romantic?" cried the little mermaid princess, Ariel, as she gazed around the school gym at the colorful decorations for the annual costume ball. Ariel, her six older sisters—Aquata, Alana, Andrina, Attina, Adella, and Arista—and several of their friends from school had volunteered to be on the decorating committee.

"Don't get too excited yet," cautioned Ariel's oldest sister, Aquata. "We're not finished with the decorating. We still have more crepe paper to hang."

"Well, I think it looks absolutely perfect already," Ariel declared. "This is definitely going to be the best costume ball the school's ever had!" She twirled around the room, pretending to waltz with an imaginary partner.

Andrina nudged her friend Breona. The two girls played together on the school's finball team. "I think Ariel needs a prince to sweep her off her tail," Andrina whispered.

"At least her imaginary partner's a good dancer," Breona said, laughing. "Unlike *my* date for the ball."

"I think Linvard's kind of charming," Andrina said. "Especially if you like lousy jokes. And at least he's a better dancer than my date, Dulin."

"Hey, that's my brother you're insulting," Breona exclaimed with a grin.

Aquata was passing out rolls of yellow-and-blue crepe paper to the rest of the mermaids. "We still need to decorate the refreshments table," she instructed.

"Oh, who cares?" Adella said impatiently.

"Once I show up in my costume, no one will be looking at the decorations, anyway."

"Have you decided what you're going to wear, Adella?" asked Ramy, one of Adella's closest friends. Ramy was always trying to get fashion tips from Adella.

"Adella's coming as her very favorite thing in the whole world," Ariel said with a laugh. "A mirror!"

"Ha-ha, very funny. You're just jealous because you don't have a date yet," Adella replied.

"I will soon," Ariel said. "I'm going to ask Gil."

"Gil's not exactly a date," Adella pointed out. "You and he are just friends."

"A friend can be a date, too," said Aquata. "Ariel has plenty of time ahead of her to worry about romance. As for me, I've asked Nexar. He's that cute new junior stagehand at the theater."

"Speaking of romance," Arista said dreamily, "I'm definitely going to ask Dylan. I just found out he's going to be in town that weekend for a family reunion. I can't wait to see him again."

"Who's Dylan?" asked Breona.

"A stableboy she met at our summer palace," Andrina explained.

"A very cute stableboy," Arista added with a deep sigh.

"Who are you taking, Alana?" Andrina asked.

"I asked Malo," Alana said, her cheeks turning lobster red. "Well, actually, I was *going* to ask him, but then I got all tongue-tied." She twisted one of her dark pigtails around her finger. "So he ended up asking me."

"But this is the Girls Ask Boys Ball," Adella scolded her shy sister. "We're *supposed* to ask out the boys. It's traditional. Of course, in my case that's not easy. There are at least five boys who are dying for me to ask them." She sighed. "Decisions, decisions."

"Still," said Ramy timidly, "I know what Alana means. It took me weeks to get up the nerve to ask Quenzell."

Adella rolled her eyes. "I *told* you not to ask that boy, Ramy," she said. "He's four inches shorter than you."

"That doesn't matter, Adella," Ariel said.

4

"Besides," Ramy said, looking a little embarrassed, "he promised to wear a very tall costume."

Attina glanced over at the door. "Well," she said casually, clearing her throat, "I'd better get over to the library if I want to get that history report done."

"Wait," Ariel said. "You haven't told us who you asked to the ball, Attina."

Attina gulped like a nervous goldfish. "Um, I haven't really thought about it," she said quickly. She handed her crepe paper to Ariel. "I have to get going. It looks like there are enough people here to handle the rest of the decorations without me."

Ariel and the others watched as Attina swam away in a flurry of bubbles. "I hope I didn't embarrass her," Ariel whispered to her sisters a moment later when Ramy and Breona were out of hearing range. "I didn't realize she doesn't have a date yet."

Arista smiled. "I wouldn't feel too sorry for Attina," she said. "I think she has a certain special person in mind."

Count on Arista to know, Ariel thought. She often noticed things others missed.

"Who is it?" Ariel asked. "Tell us, Arista!"

Arista glanced at the door to make sure that Attina had left. "Well, I'm not sure *exactly* who it is. But you may have noticed that Attina has been spending a lot of time at the public library lately."

Adella nodded. "Sure. We all know what a bookworm she is."

"Well, yesterday I overheard her talking to her friend Nell about a very good-looking boy who just happens to work part-time at the library," Arista said. "She said he's new in town."

"So she's been holding out on us!" Adella cried.

"You already have *five* boys you're interested in," Aquata pointed out. "You don't need a sixth."

"Still," Adella said, "we can at least go and get a look at this mystery man, can't we?"

"First we finish decorating this gym," Aquata insisted.

"Then we go and spy?" Adella asked hopefully.

All the mermaids grinned.

"*Then* we go and spy," Aquata agreed.

6

As Attina swam toward the library, Ariel's words were still ringing in her ears. *You haven't told us who you asked to the ball, Attina.*

If only she had an answer! No one would believe that she was afraid to ask a boy on a date. After all, she was a royal princess. People expected her to be popular and outgoing. Sometimes she wished she could just be an ordinary mermaid and not have to live up to anyone's expectations.

She swam into the library and glanced

hopefully toward the front desk. Sure enough, Tedrick was there, arranging a load of books on a cart. He paused and opened a book of poems by Sharkspeare. As he read silently, his eyes misted over, and he let out a long sigh.

Attina sighed, too. It was easy to see how sensitive and intelligent Tedrick was. He wasn't like the other boys she knew.

She drifted over to a table, sat down, and pulled out her history textbook and a notebook. Opening the book, Attina started to read the assignment on Joan of the Arctic. But soon her eyes strayed from the book back to Tedrick. He had stopped reading, too. In fact, he seemed to be staring in her direction. But when she caught his eyes, he quickly turned away. He moved so suddenly that he slammed into his book cart.

Yesterday, Tedrick had banged into the teacher's desk while he was reading one of his own poems in front of the class. Some of the kids had snickered—but not Attina. She had been overwhelmed by the beauty of Tedrick's poem and by the heartfelt way he had read it.

If only she could write that well. Then maybe Tedrick would notice her. Attina opened her notebook and picked up her pencil. She wrote carefully, trying out each word in her mind before writing it down.

I sat and thought of thee
In my room through half the night,
While the current moved so slow,
And the starfish glimmered bright.

I sit and think of thee,
And I know in all the oceans,
No other boy can cause me
To feel such warm emotions.

When she had finished, Attina read over her poem again. It was a little like a famous poem by Percy Bisque Shellfish. She knew it wasn't nearly as good as the poem Tedrick had written. Still, she thought, it wasn't bad for a first try.

Attina gazed over at Tedrick. He was talking to his cousin Taz, who also worked part-time at the library. It's strange, Attina thought. They look a lot alike, but their personalities seem very different. Of course, since both boys had just moved to town, she didn't know either one very well. But she had the feeling that Taz was a bit conceited. Tedrick, on the other hand, was sensitive and sweet and brilliant and . . .

Tedrick, Tedrick, Tedrick. If only she had the nerve to ask him to the costume ball. But she was afraid that someone as deep as he obviously was wouldn't be interested in someone like her.

Just then she noticed a swirl of activity as her sisters swam in. Attina quickly slammed her notebook shut. She'd die if any of her sisters ever knew she was writing romantic poems about a boy!

Especially a boy who didn't even know she existed.

* * *

Ariel waved to her sister, but Attina had her head buried in her history book. "Do you see the boy Attina has her eye on?" Ariel whispered to Arista.

Arista gazed around the library. "See those two boys behind the checkout desk? It must be one of them."

Ariel nodded. "Do you know who they are?"

"The cool-looking one is Taz," Arista said. "Just about every girl in school is interested in him. In addition to being the best-looking boy in town, I hear he's also really friendly and easygoing. The other one's his cousin. He's named Hedrick, or Dedrick, or Frederick, or something. Their parents just moved here. They're helping to construct the new addition to the palace."

"They look a lot alike," said Andrina.

"I wonder which one Attina is interested in," Aquata said in a low whisper.

Just then Tedrick tripped over his tail and plowed into a pile of books on the counter. The stack of books toppled and fell over, crashing to the floor. As Tedrick bent over to pick up the books, he banged his head against the edge of the counter. Taz rolled his eyes. Reluctantly he reached down to give his cousin a hand.

"I think I can guess," Adella said, giving Taz a long look. "At least," she said with a smile, "I know which one *I* would be interested in."

Later that evening, after a delicious dinner of plankton soup and kelp salad, the princesses gathered in the palace library to work on their homework. At least, *some* of them were studying. Adella was busy trying out a fashionable new hair braid she'd seen in *Mademoishelle* magazine. And Andrina was tossing paper balls across the room into a conch-shell wastebasket.

"Two points!" she cried when one went

in. She tried another, but it bounced off the top of Attina's head.

"Sorry, Attina," she said.

"Actually, I'm the one who's sorry," Attina said. "I should have helped you guys finish decorating the gym today."

"That's okay," said Aquata. "There wasn't that much left to do."

"Besides," Adella said with a wink, "we know you had more important things to worry about."

"I did have a lot of research to do," Attina said.

"Research?" Adella laughed. "Yes, but what was the subject? Could it have been a certain handsome boy we noticed at the checkout desk?"

Attina blushed. "I don't know what you're talking about. I was studying history."

"Uh-huh," Adella said skeptically, still playing with her braid. "It looked to me as though you were studying the history of a certain boy."

"Stop teasing her," Ariel scolded. "If she doesn't want to talk about it, that's fine."

"Well, she'd better do something soon,"

Arista said. "The dance is only a few days away, and she still doesn't have a date."

"I know how Attina feels," Alana said softly. "I hate this whole girls-ask-boys thing. But you just have to get up your courage and do it."

"Oh please, a little more subtlety," Adella chided. "You don't just *ask* a boy out. You have to flirt a little first."

Aquata rolled her eyes. "And you would be the expert on that, Adella," she said with a smile.

"You're right, I *am* the expert," Adella said. She gave up on her braid and swam over to Attina. "Flirting is easy, once you get the hang of it. There's just one thing to remember—eye contact."

"Eye contact?" Attina echoed.

"Your eyes meet his, and unspoken messages travel between you," Adella said. "Watch me." She looked Attina in the eyes, then let her lids droop a little. "See?"

"How can you see anything with your eyes closed like that?" Attina asked.

Adella sighed. "Just try it the next time you want to get your cute friend from the

library to look at you. And while you're at it, don't forget to pout your lips." She pursed her lips together.

Ariel giggled. "You look like a squid, Adella."

"If that's what it takes to get a guy to notice me, it's not worth it," Attina said grumpily. "I refuse to walk around school with my lips puffed up and my eyes closed just to get a date for some stupid dance." She reached for her history book. "I'm going to my room, where I can concentrate. You can all waste your time worrying about batting your eyes. I have more interesting things to think about."

"Poor Attina," Adella whispered as she watched her sister swim away. "I don't think she'll ever get up the nerve to ask Taz to the ball."

"I wish there was some way we could get them together," said Andrina as she crumpled another piece of paper and tossed it over Ariel's head and into the basket. She reached for the notebook that Attina had left lying on the table. "Do you think Attina will mind if I borrow a couple of sheets of her paper?"

"No," said Ariel. "But I do think she might mind if we try to fix her up with Taz. Wouldn't that be kind of embarrassing?"

"Definitely embarrassing," Alana agreed. "It makes *me* blush just thinking about it."

Andrina laughed. "*Everything* makes you blush, Alana."

"Maybe we could find a nonembarrassing way to do it," Arista said. "If we thought it over logically, I'm sure we could come up with a plan."

"Hey, wait a minute," Andrina said. She tapped the open notebook in front of her. "I think I may have stumbled across the perfect way to get Taz's attention."

Adella frowned. "Better than eye batting?"

"Much better. This is Attina's notebook," Andrina said. "And she's written a poem in it."

"She's always writing something," Adella said.

Andrina raised an eyebrow. "Not love poems. And this sure sounds like a love poem to me."

"Read it out loud," Adella urged.

"I don't think we should," said Aquata.

"It wouldn't be right." She paused. "Unless, of course, you've already *accidentally* read it, Andrina. In which case it wouldn't exactly be as sneaky."

"Wait a minute," Alana objected. "I don't think we should be prying into Attina's love life."

Adella laughed. "Attina doesn't *have* a love life. Not yet. Maybe this poem will give us an idea how to help her get one."

"I don't know, Adella," Ariel said doubtfully. "What if we try to help and something goes wrong? You should never interfere with true love. If Attina and Taz are meant to be together, it will happen."

Adella rolled her eyes. "Ariel, you are such a romantic! Don't get your tail all bent out of shape. We're just going to give Attina a helping hand."

Andrina cleared her throat. "Here it is," she said. "The poem I just happened to *accidentally* read."

The mermaids listened quietly while Andrina read Attina's poem out loud.

"Wow," Ariel said dreamily when Andrina was through. "I wish *I* liked a boy well enough to write him poems like that." She sighed. "I hope I will someday."

"Too bad Attina can't just say all those things to Taz," said Arista.

"Too bad he can't just read the poem," Aquata said.

"Exactly what I was thinking," Adella said, a devilish gleam in her eyes. "And maybe he can. I believe I may just have come up with a brilliant plan."

"Uh-oh," said Aquata. "I don't trust your brilliant plans, Adella."

Adella swished her tail impatiently. "Don't worry, Aquata. This plan is foolproof. Here's step one—we need to make a copy of that poem."

4

"I can't believe that none of us has a single library book," Adella complained after school the next day. "We need a library book or my brilliant plan will never work."

"Stupid plan, you mean," Ariel said, shaking her head.

"It's not a stupid plan," Adella replied. "It's going to work like a charm. Arista convinced Attina to go sea horse riding this afternoon. Now all we have to do is go to the library and return a book—"

"Except that we can't *return* a book because none of us *has* a book," Andrina reminded her.

Aquata snapped her fingers. "Father always has a pile of library books in his den. We can use one of those."

"Perfect!" Adella said. "Let's go."

The princesses swam straight to King Triton's den. It was a big room full of huge chairs and heavy tables with coral legs carved to look like dolphins, sharks, and other sea creatures.

"There!" Ariel said. She pointed to a pile of books on a small, round table beside Triton's favorite chair.

Aquata picked up one of the books. "*Remembrance of Things Sunk*, by Mackerel Proust," she read. "There's no way Taz is going to believe this is Attina's book."

"How about this one?" Adella said. She held up a book entitled *The Poetry of Alfred, Lord Tunason*.

"That will have to do," Aquata said. "At least it's a book of poems."

Adella pulled a piece of paper out of her book bag and smoothed it out with her hands. Then she slipped the paper inside the book. "Now for the second part of the plan!"

The mermaids swam out of the palace and hurried toward the library. When they arrived, they saw that Taz was working behind the checkout desk and Tedrick was shelving books.

"Good, Taz is here," Adella said. She sighed wistfully. "He *is* cute, isn't he? I must say, it really is awfully nice of me to be such a good sister and try to get him interested in Attina."

Alana looked worried. "I know we're doing all this for Attina's own good, but I still can't help thinking she's going to be pretty upset when she finds out."

"Alana's right," Ariel said. "We all know how sensitive Attina is. She'd be humiliated if people thought she didn't have the guts to ask Taz to the dance face-to-face. I think we should forget about this ridiculous plan while we still can."

"No way, Ariel," Aquata said. "We've got to help Attina or she'll never get together with Taz. But you do have a point about people finding out. Maybe we should add something to the poem telling Taz to keep it a secret just between them."

Adella shrugged. "Whatever." She handed Aquata the book. "Here it is. Add whatever you want."

Aquata opened the book and reread the poem. "You did a good job making this look like Attina's handwriting," she commented. Suddenly she frowned. "But what's this?" She pointed to a verse that had been added to the end of the poem:

Please accept my plea
And say you'll come with me
To the best dance in the sea.
I hope you will agree!
Signed, Princess Attina

"It doesn't really go very well with the rest of the poem," Arista said doubtfully. "And isn't it a little obvious?"

"I added that part because I didn't want there to be any mistakes," Adella explained.

"I thought you said this plan was foolproof," said Alana.

"Of course it is," Adella said confidently. "I'll go up to Taz and hand him this book. I'll tell him that Attina checked it out and she wanted me to return it for her. Then he'll notice the poem and read it. Naturally, he'll think Attina wrote it and left it in the book for him to find."

"I definitely think we should ask him to keep it a secret," Alana said. "This whole plan sounds totally embarrassing if you ask me."

"Well, let's go ahead and add whatever we're going to add and get on with it," Adella said impatiently. She found a pen in the bottom of her book bag and handed it to Aquata.

"Okay," Aquata said. "How about just putting 'P.S.—please don't tell *anyone* about our date.'"

Adella frowned. "Won't that sound a little weird? He might think she's ashamed of him or something."

Arista laughed. "Somehow I get the impression that possibility wouldn't even occur to Taz."

Aquata quickly jotted the line beneath

Attina's name, then showed it to Ariel and Alana. "There. Does that make you two happy?"

"That's better, I guess," Ariel said. "Although, just for the record, I still say we shouldn't try to play matchmaker."

"Watch," Adella said. "This will all work out perfectly."

"Just promise me this," Ariel said. "When *I* fall madly in love with the perfect guy, I don't want you guys cooking up any complicated secret plans to get us together, OK?"

Adella shook her head. "And just who is this perfect guy? Gil?"

"Oh, no. You know Gil's just a good friend." Ariel sighed. "My perfect guy will be handsome—"

"Of course," Adella said.

"And brave."

"Naturally," Andrina agreed, smiling.

"And he'll make me laugh."

"Always a good idea," Aquata said. "Do you have any other requirements?"

Ariel nodded slyly. "He'll be from out of town. *Way* out of town."

"I don't know about that," said Arista with a sigh. "I hardly ever get to see Dylan."

"But you see, if he's from out of town," Ariel continued with a grin, "I won't have to worry about any of you concocting some crazy matchmaking scheme!"

The princesses swam over to the library checkout desk with Adella in the lead. Taz looked up and smiled as they approached. He certainly *was* handsome, Ariel had to admit.

Adella batted her eyes. "Hi," she said. "I'm Adella."

"I've seen you around," Taz said cheerfully. "You're one of the King's daughters, aren't you?"

Adella nodded. "Yes, but you don't have to bow or anything. Even though I'm a beautiful princess, I'm really just your basic, normal girl inside." She paused to pout her lips. Andrina elbowed her in the side. "Oh," Adella said, unpuckering. "These are four of my sisters: Ariel, Alana, Andrina, and Aquata."

Taz ran his fingers through his wavy hair. When he smiled, his teeth gleamed like a row of pearls. "Glad to meet you," he said. "I make it a point to meet all the best-looking girls."

Ariel rolled her eyes. Taz seemed more than a little stuck-up to her.

"Isn't that a coincidence," said Adella. She twirled a lock of hair around her finger. "I make it a point to meet all the best-looking boys!"

Ariel poked her in the shoulder. "Adella, don't you have something you want to say?"

"What?" Adella said. "Oh, right." Reluctantly she handed the book to Taz. "Here. My sister *Attina* wanted me to return this. She couldn't come today. But *Attina* checked it out, and she wanted me to be sure and return it to *you*."

"OK," Taz said with a shrug.

"Don't forget, Attina wanted *you* to have it," Ariel added as Taz took the book.

The mermaids swam slowly away. When they reached the door, they paused to glance back at Taz. He was putting the book on a cart.

"Oh no!" Aquata whispered. "He didn't see the note!"

Suddenly Taz frowned. He opened the book and pulled out a sheet of paper.

"He's reading it!" Andrina cried.

Taz ran his fingers through his hair again. As he read, he nodded as if he agreed with everything the poem had to say. Then he looked around and caught sight of the princesses. He smiled confidently and gave them a big wink.

"Message delivered," Ariel said. "I guess your plan worked after all, Adella."

"What did I tell you?" Adella said. She gazed at Taz and sighed. "Foolproof."

"Have any of you seen a book called *The Poetry of Alfred, Lord Tunason?*" King Triton asked at dinner that evening. "I was sure it was in my den, and now I can't seem to find it."

"I haven't seen it, Father," Attina answered. She noticed that Adella nearly choked on her sponge cake. Her other sisters all seemed to be very busy concentrating on their own desserts.

Dover, the King's head butler, entered the

dining room. Dover was a very dignified merman from the English Channel.

"There is a young gentleman at the door," he said.

"Well, what does he want?" Triton asked. "It's dinnertime, Dover."

"He says he would like to see Princess Attina," Dover replied.

Attina felt her heart skip a beat. A boy was here to see her? There must be some mistake.

"Attina?" King Triton said in surprise. "Usually it's Adella's boyfriends who come barging in here at all the wrong times." He turned to Attina. "Well, who is this young man?"

"I . . . I don't know," Attina admitted. "May I be excused to go see?"

The King raised one bushy eyebrow. "I suppose so. But be sure to tell that young man not to interrupt my dessert again."

Dover cleared his throat. "Where would you like to receive the young man, Princess?"

"I'll wait for him in the parlor," Attina said nervously.

The other mermaids watched Attina follow

31

Dover down the hall toward the parlor. "Father," said Aquata, "I don't suppose we could—"

"Oh, so now you *all* have to go?" Triton asked. He sighed. "Fine. You're excused."

The princesses zoomed from the dining hall. They gathered in the parlor, where the King often entertained guests. Attina sat in a giant clamshell stuffed with sea green cushions. Her sisters lined up side by side on the couches on either side of the clamshell.

"Shall I send the young gentleman in?" Dover asked Attina.

Attina gulped. "Are you sure he asked for *me*, Dover?"

"Yes, Princess."

"Hurry up, Attina!" Andrina urged. "We're dying of curiosity."

"Yes, Attina, let's see this admirer of yours," Adella said.

Attina turned to Dover. "OK, you can have him come in now, please."

"Yes, Princess," the butler said.

He disappeared around the corner. Attina waited nervously. Her heart was fluttering. Who could it be? Part of her dared to hope it was Tedrick. But she knew that that wasn't very likely. After all, Tedrick didn't even know she was alive. She'd barely said two words to him.

Maybe he had read the look in her eyes. After all, he was very sensitive. Maybe he'd guessed her true feelings.

There was a stir and Dover reappeared, followed by a merboy whose face was concealed behind a bouquet of pink water lilies. Attina held her breath. It was him—it had to be him!

The boy lowered the flowers. But it wasn't Tedrick's sweet, sensitive face that appeared. This boy's face was far more self-confident.

"I guess you were expecting me," Taz said. He handed her the flowers.

"Expecting you?" Attina asked in amazement.

"Sure, babe. I mean, sure, Princess," Taz said.

"Well," Attina admitted, "not really."

"Oh, I get it," Taz said. "You figured because I'm so popular and you're, well, kind of quiet that I wouldn't want to go to the dance with you."

"What?" Attina cried.

"Of course I'll take you to the dance," Taz said. "I mean, plenty of girls have asked me out before, but the way you did it was so totally cool and original."

Attina felt her mouth drop open. "It was?"

"Sure, babe." Taz paused to admire his reflection in the mirror behind the couch. "I mean, Princess. And don't worry, I'll keep it a secret. I guess you want to make a big splash when we swim in together, huh?"

Attina looked over at her sisters. For some reason, they were all grinning from ear to ear. *I have no idea what's going on,* she wanted to say. But she was too polite to embarrass Taz.

"I'm thinking about going as a killer whale," Taz said. "The meanest, toughest creature in the ocean."

"I'm going as a flying fish," Adella cut in. "I have a great costume with big, shimmering wings."

Attina sighed. She was trapped. She didn't know Taz, and she had a feeling that if she did, she wouldn't like him very much. But there was no polite way to say no to him

35

now. "I guess I'll go as a seal," she said at last.

Taz frowned. "Hmm. A killer whale and a seal? They don't exactly go together. Couldn't you go as something really mean? You know, like a barracuda?"

"Well," Attina said hesitantly, "I'm not really the barracuda type."

"Hey, no prob. You be a seal, I'll be a killer whale." He winked at her. "You know what they say—opposites attract."

"Yes," Attina said politely. "That's what they say, all right."

"Congratulations," Aquata said after Taz had left. She patted Attina on the back. "See? Now you have a date for the big dance."

"And a good-looking date, too," Adella said a little wistfully. "Taz is so charming. I'm sure you'll have a great time."

"I'm glad it all worked out the way you wanted it to, Attina," Alana said.

"Thanks to me," Adella said proudly. "After all, it was *my* brilliant plan."

Attina narrowed her eyes. "Your plan?"

"Absolutely," Adella said.

"Hey, *I* found the poem," Andrina said. "Without the poem, the whole thing would never have worked."

"*What* poem?" Attina asked.

"Your poem," Adella said. "You know. The mushy one. Glimmering starfish? Warm emotions?"

Attina felt her face growing hot. "You read that?"

"We read it, then we copied it," Adella said.

"You read *my* poem?" Attina demanded, her voice rising.

"That's how we got Taz to go out with you," Adella explained proudly. "We made a copy of your poem and slipped it to him. Of course, I had to add a line or two about how much you wanted Taz to go to the dance with you."

"You just went right up and gave my poem to *Taz?*" Attina cried in horror.

"We were a little more subtle than that," said Adella.

Andrina nodded. "We knew you liked

him," she said. "But since you were too shy to ask him out, we decided to take care of it for you."

"Aren't you relieved?" Alana asked.

"Relieved?" Attina shrieked. "How could I be relieved? Now I'm stuck going out with that stuck-up guy!"

"But isn't Taz the guy you've been mooning over?" Aquata asked, looking confused. "I mean, he doesn't seem much like your type, but he *is* good-looking, and he seems like he could be a lot of fun. . . ."

"Me, mooning over Taz? No way!" Attina wailed. "He's not the one. Taz isn't sensitive or intelligent or poetic. He's just vain and shallow."

"Wait a minute," Andrina said. "Time out. Are you saying you're *not* interested in Taz?"

Attina threw up her hands. "That's exactly what I'm saying! That poem wasn't for Taz. If you must know, it was for Tedrick."

"Tedrick?" Andrina echoed.

"The one who keeps tripping over his own tail?" Alana said.

"The one who bangs into furniture?" Arista asked.

"The one who's not nearly as popular as Taz?" Adella added.

"I don't care if he's not popular," Attina said. "That's not important."

Adella looked confused. "It's not?"

"I can't believe this," Andrina said. "Who'd ever have guessed that Attina likes Tedrick?"

Alana signed. "Too bad she's going to the dance with his cousin."

"Maybe you could just tell Taz it was all a mistake, Attina," Aquata suggested.

Attina shook her head. "I can't embarrass him just because my nosy sisters messed everything up," she said sadly. "I'll just have to try to make the best of it." She started to swim away, her head hung low. Then she turned to look back at her sisters. "Only do me one favor."

Ariel nodded. "Anything."

"Don't do me any more favors," Attina said.

"I don't think your brilliant plan is working out very well, Adella," Ariel said. "As a matter of fact, I don't think it's working out at all."

"That's the understatement of the year," Andrina added.

The mermaids were upstairs in Aquata's room. Attina was off by herself in her own bedroom.

"At least Attina has a date for the costume ball," Adella said defensively. "I've been so busy with my plan that I haven't even had a chance to decide who to ask myself yet."

"Too bad she's going with a guy she doesn't like," said Ariel.

"Too bad she's going with a guy I *do* like," Adella grumbled. She shrugged. "Well, what's done is done."

"What do you mean?" Aquata demanded. "You can't just leave things this way."

"I can't?" Adella said. She swam over to her mirror, smoothing her scales while she thought for a moment. "OK," she said at last. "Let's try Plan B."

"I'm almost afraid to ask this," Ariel said. "What's Plan B?"

"We write a *second* poem," Adella said excitedly. "Then we pretend it's from Attina and give it to Tedrick."

Arista groaned. "That sounds just like Plan A."

"It is, except this time we do it right," said Adella. "This time it will be Tedrick who Attina is asking out."

"What about Taz?" Alana asked. "He thinks he's going out with Attina."

"No problem," Adella said breezily. "I'll

simply step in and, out of the goodness of my heart, ask Taz to go with me."

"Very noble of you," Ariel said dryly.

"There's one problem," Arista said. "Who's going to write this new poem?"

Adella shrugged. "We can all work on it together. How hard could it be to write one tiny little poem? Someone grab a sheet of paper, and let's get started."

Aquata found paper and a pen, and the mermaids gathered around her. "OK," Aquata said expectantly, holding the pen. "Somebody start."

The princesses stared at each other. No one said a word.

Aquata pointed to Arista. "You always get good grades. This should be easy for you."

"I don't know anything about writing poetry," Arista protested.

"It just has to rhyme," Adella said impatiently. "And be romantic."

"How about *Tedrick, you're cool; Tedrick, you're tall. Please go with me to the big costume ball?*" Andrina said.

Aquata shook her head. "Very weak, Andrina."

"I still think we should just leave well enough alone," Ariel said. "True love can't be arranged. It just happens."

Suddenly Aquata started writing on the sheet of paper.

"What are you writing?" Arista asked.

Aquata held out the sheet and read what she'd jotted down.

There once was a cute boy named Tedrick.

"Wonderful," Adella commented sarcastically. "Good luck trying to find something to rhyme with *Tedrick.*"

"Ice pick," Alana suggested.

"Redbrick," said Ariel.

Aquata crumpled up the paper and threw it away. "Let's try again." On a fresh sheet of paper she wrote:

There once was a shy, lovesick poet

She looked up. "That's Attina," she explained.

"Now we're getting somewhere," said Adella.

"How about this?" said Alana. She cleared her throat:

There once was a shy, lovesick poet
Who didn't quite know how to show it.
   She wanted the chance
   To go to the dance,
But the boy whom she loved didn't know it.

"Excellent!" Adella cried.

"Very moving," Andrina agreed.

Aquata finished writing down the poem and handed the sheet of paper to Adella.

"See?" Adella said as she admired the poem. "Plan B is already off to a good start. First thing tomorrow morning, I'll make sure Tedrick gets this." She grinned. "Trust me on this one. It's foolproof."

8

The next afternoon the princesses had their lesson with Sebastian, the royal court composer. Unfortunately Sebastian was in an especially crabby mood.

"No, no, no!" he cried in frustration. "You aren't paying attention. It's la-la-*LA*-la, not la-*LA*-la-la."

"Sorry, Sebastian," Ariel said. "We'll try to pay better attention."

"Good," Sebastian grumbled. "Now, once again." He raised his baton.

Dover appeared in the music room doorway. "Pardon—"

"No!" Sebastian yelled. "No interruptions."

"But there are two gentlemen callers waiting in the parlor," Dover said.

"I don't care if there's a pair of great white sharks!" Sebastian cried. He paused, frowning. "There *aren't* any great white sharks, are there?" he added nervously.

"Just two young gentlemen," Dover repeated.

"Tell them to wait," Sebastian ordered.

"But Sebastian," Adella complained, "this could be very important!"

"Nothing is more important than your lessons," Sebastian said firmly. "Now, all together." Once again he raised his baton.

The mermaids all exchanged a quick glance. "La-*LA*-la-la," they sang.

"No, no, no!" Sebastian cried. "How many times must I tell you? Emphasize the third *LA*."

"I guess we're a little distracted," Ariel said.

"Our minds must be somewhere else," Adella agreed.

"Harrumph," Sebastian said. "In other words, you won't pay attention until I let you go and see who these gentlemen callers are?"

"Maybe it would be better if we just got rid of those boys first," Aquata suggested. "Then we could *really* concentrate."

Sebastian waved his baton at them angrily. "I will have to tell the King that his daughters are all becoming boy crazy."

He shooed them away. All the mermaids dashed toward the door—all except Attina, who drifted along slowly and aimlessly in their wake.

"Now, remember the plan," Adella whispered to her other sisters when she was certain Attina couldn't hear. "Tedrick accepts Attina's invitation. Naturally Attina will be confused. She'll probably start to say something about how she's already promised to go with Taz. That's when I'll step in and volunteer to go with Taz myself."

"Dover said there were *two* guys," said Arista.

"Maybe Tedrick brought along a friend for moral support," Alana suggested.

"Are you sure Tedrick saw the poem we wrote?" Aquata asked in a whisper.

"Positive," Adella replied. "I put it in a library book. Then I gave the book directly to him."

"Did you say anything to him?" Andrina asked Adella. "You know, about Attina?"

"Since she signed Attina's name to the poem, she didn't have to say anything," Ariel said. "Tedrick must have assumed it was from Attina."

Suddenly Adella frowned. "Signed Attina's name?"

"You did sign Attina's name, didn't you?" Ariel asked.

"Um, I think I did," Adella said nervously. "In fact, I'm sure. Almost."

* * *

When Attina entered the parlor with her sisters, the first person she saw was Taz. Then she saw his companion standing awkwardly by the door. She gasped. Tedrick was here to see her! He was holding flowers in his hand, just as Taz had done. But Tedrick was clutching the bouquet of water lilies so hard that all the stems had snapped.

"Hi, Tedrick," Attina said shyly. "What are you doing here?"

"I'm, um, here about the, um, the costume ball," Tedrick answered. He stared at the floor, digging the tip of his tail beneath the edge of the carpet.

Suddenly Tedrick thrust the flowers forward. "Here," he said.

Attina's heart did a little somersault. "Thank—," she started to say.

"These are for you, Princess Adella," Tedrick continued.

Attina's jaw dropped open. *Adella?* Tedrick was here to see Adella?

Attina spun around. Adella's face was as white as a fish belly.

"For—for me?" Adella said in a hoarse whisper.

"Your poem was so . . . so moving, Adella," Tedrick said. "I wasn't expecting to go to the ball, but since you asked, and in such a nice way—"

"But—but—," Adella spluttered.

"Anyway," Tedrick said uncomfortably, "I accept your invitation to the ball." He turned to leave and ran smack into a coral statue of the King, almost knocking it over. Dover rushed over and caught it in the nick of time.

"What did I tell you, Tedrick?" Taz said, slapping his cousin on the back. "No need to be nervous." He winked at Attina as he and Tedrick were leaving the room. "See you on the big night, babe."

9

"Brilliant plan," Attina said mockingly.

"I was just trying to help!" Adella cried.

"I'd have thought you would have learned your lesson after your first stupid plan," Attina said. "The plan that left me stuck with Taz."

"And now *I'm* stuck with Tedrick," Adella said gloomily. "That's much worse."

"It is not!" Attina cried. "Tedrick is sweet and brilliant, and best of all, he doesn't call me *babe*. Of course, now he probably thinks

I'm an idiot." She waved the second poem in Adella's face. "This poem is pathetic. I'm glad he doesn't think *I* wrote it. I would never write anything this bad."

"Well! That's the last time I ever try to help *you* out," Adella snapped. She turned her back and swam away.

"I hope that's a promise!" Attina shouted after her. Then she swam off toward her room.

Ariel watched them go, shaking her head in dismay. "What a mess."

"This costume ball was supposed to be fun," Alana said. "Now everyone is mad, and no one's going to have a good time."

"What if we just went to Taz and Tedrick and told them the truth?" Arista asked logically.

Aquata shook her head. "What would we say? We'd have to admit how sneaky we were being. And Attina would be so totally embarrassed."

"Besides," Andrina pointed out, "what if Taz really prefers Attina and Tedrick prefers Adella? If we try to change it back around, their feelings could be hurt."

"But Taz is so right for Adella and so wrong for Attina," Arista said. "And Tedrick is just right for Attina but totally wrong for Adella."

"Stop! You're making my head spin," Ariel cried.

"Who knows?" Aquata said philosophically. "Maybe after both couples spend some time together, they'll find they actually like each other."

Suddenly a very sneaky idea popped into Ariel's head. "You know," she said, "the boys won't even be able to recognize Adella and Attina in their costumes."

"So?" Aquata asked.

"So, what if Adella and Attina *switch* costumes?"

All the mermaids were silent for a moment. Andrina was the first to speak. "Taz will be looking for a girl dressed in a seal costume. And Tedrick will be looking for a girl dressed as a flying fish. Attina and Adella are about the same height, and their voices are pretty similar . . ."

"And their hair will be covered by their costumes," Ariel finished.

"So Taz would be with Adella," Alana said, "even though he'll think he's with Attina."

"And Tedrick would be with Attina, even though he'll think he's with Adella," Arista added.

"Everyone would have a good time," Aquata said thoughtfully. "But what happens at midnight when we all take off our masks?"

"Then the boys will learn the truth," Ariel said. "But by then it won't matter. They'll realize they were each with the right girl all along."

"Nobody's feelings would be hurt," Arista said.

"And everything would work out perfectly after all," Ariel said.

"Who's going to convince Adella and Attina to switch costumes?" Aquata asked.

"I will," Ariel said.

"I don't know," Arista said doubtfully. "I think Attina is sick and tired of people making plans that involve her."

"She's just tired of Adella's plans," Ariel said confidently. "This is *my* plan. And it's going to work."

Aquata shook her head. "I thought you didn't believe in interfering in other people's love lives."

"We've already interfered," Ariel replied. "This is *un*interfering." She grinned. "And it's foolproof."

* * *

Taz and Tedrick swam away from the palace, toward their homes. Both merboys were very quiet. For Tedrick that was normal. But Taz usually loved to talk, even when no one was listening.

"What's bugging you, Taz?" Tedrick asked finally.

Taz shrugged. "Nothing. How about you?"

Tedrick shook his head. "Nothing's bothering me, either."

They swam past a ridge of pink coral. "Attina's pretty, isn't she?" Taz said.

"Very," Tedrick said enthusiastically. "Er, I mean, sure, I guess so."

"Of course," Taz added, "she's no Adella."

Tedrick glanced over at him. "I think Attina's great. Not only is she beautiful, she's smart and sensitive, too."

Taz laughed. "I don't care all that much

about smartness and sensitivity. I like a girl who's popular and lots of fun."

"Like Adella?" Tedrick asked.

Taz shrugged again. "You're lucky to be going out with her."

"You want to know the truth, Cousin?" Tedrick said. "I'd rather be going out with Attina. I think we'd be perfect for each other."

Taz gasped. "I'd rather be going out with Adella. She's just my kind of girl."

"Wait a minute," Tedrick said. "It sounds to me as though we're going out with the wrong girls."

"I guess so," Taz admitted. "Too bad there's nothing we can do about it."

"It would hurt their feelings if we told Adella and Attina we wanted to switch," Tedrick said.

"You're probably right. But it's too bad, because I know I'd have a better time with Adella. And no offense, Cousin, but I'm sure Adella would have a better time with me."

Tedrick nodded glumly. They swam for a while in silence. Suddenly a wonderful idea popped into Tedrick's head. "Maybe there *is* a way we can each go out with the right girl, after all," he said slyly.

10

The evening of the ball, the princesses gathered in the parlor to await the arrival of their dates.

"I'm so nervous!" cried Arista as she swam around the room. She swam over to a mirror and gazed anxiously into it. "Do you think Dylan will like my costume?"

"You look just like a real sea horse," Ariel assured her.

"I'm supposed to look like Foamy," Arista said. Foamy was her favorite sea horse at the royal stables. She had told Dylan all about him.

"Would you quit swimming around in circles!" Adella complained as she pushed Arista aside to examine her own reflection in the mirror. "Your bubbles are messing up my whiskers." She adjusted her mask, which had a cute seal smile and long bushy whiskers.

"I'm still not sure this plan of yours is going to work," Attina said to Ariel, who was dressed as a giant starfish.

"What could go wrong, Attina?" Ariel asked. "Even I can't recognize you in that flying fish costume."

"I guess you're right," Attina said.

"It *is* a great costume," Adella said grumpily. "Of course, it was supposed to be *my* costume. Instead I'm stuck dressing up as a seal." She lifted her mask and scowled. "This is such a babyish costume, Attina."

"I happen to like seals," said Attina. "And look on the bright side. By dressing this way, at least we'll each get to be with the boy we really like." She straightened her shimmering wings.

Dover appeared in the doorway. "Ahem," he said loudly. He gazed at the mermaids in their costumes and shook his head, smiling ever so slightly. "I must say, Princesses, you look most . . . well, most eye-catching." He nodded toward the entranceway. "There's a young—," he cleared his throat, "there's a young sea horse at the door. Or perhaps I should say a young gentleman in a sea horse costume. He asked me to tell you that Current has arrived."

"Current!" Arista exclaimed. "That's the name of Dylan's favorite sea horse!" She swam past Dover in a flurry of bubbles, nearly knocking him over, to meet Dylan as he entered.

"Dylan!" Arista cried. She gave him a hug. "I've missed you so much!"

Dylan laughed. "I thought I'd surprise you with this costume, but I see you had the same idea." He extended his arm. "Shall we, Foamy?"

"You know what?" Arista whispered as they left the room. "I'd rather go riding than dancing!"

"How about if we do both?" Dylan

62

suggested. "We'll go to the ball, then leave early and go for a nice long ride."

Ariel watched through a window as Dylan and Arista swam to a waiting sea conch carriage. "Isn't that sweet?" she said. "Arista and Dylan are going to have such a wonderful time tonight."

Adella and Attina exchanged a glance. "I hope *we* do, too," Adella said, twirling her seal whiskers.

"Look," Ariel exclaimed. "There's Taz!"

Adella swam to the window. "He's dressed as a killer whale, just like he said. Cool costume."

"And there's Tedrick," Attina said. "In the otter costume. He looks so cute."

"See the guy behind them?" Ariel said, pointing. "The one in the walrus costume with the long, shiny teeth? I think that's Gil."

There was a knock at the palace door, and Dover went to answer it. "Well," Ariel said, "are you two ready?"

"Ready as we'll ever be," Adella said doubtfully.

"Trust me," Ariel said. "Everything will

be fine. When *I* come up with a plan, it really works."

*   *   *

By the time the princesses arrived with their dates at the gym, it was already filled with merboys and mermaids in fantastic, colorful costumes. There were dolphins, crabs, sharks, and whales. There were lobsters and eels and fish of all kinds. One merboy who was always getting into trouble had even dressed as a devilfish.

While the band played, couples danced. Some danced near the floor. Some danced near the ceiling. Some drifted off into corners to talk or to hold hands. Others hung around a long table filled with kelp cookies, pink sea urchin punch, and other treats.

After Ariel had danced with Gil for a while, they paused to have some cookies and punch. She gazed around the gym with satisfaction. Everyone seemed to be having a good time. Andrina and Dulin spun around the room, laughing every time Dulin ran into someone. Aquata and Nexar were sitting in a corner, giggling and whispering. Alana and Malo were dancing slowly, smiling shyly at each other.

"Look," Ariel said to Gil, pointing at Adella's friend Ramy, who was dressed as an angelfish. Next to her swam Quenzell. He was dressed as a hammerhead shark, complete with a very large hammer-shaped headpiece. "Quenzell's actually taller than Ramy now!"

Arista and Dylan swam past. "Having fun?" Gil asked.

Arista nodded. "But we're tired of dancing. We're going to swim over to the stables and go for a ride."

"That'll be quite a sight!" Ariel said, laughing. "Two sea horses riding two sea horses!"

She waved good-bye to Arista and Dylan and gave Gil a nudge. "Come on," Ariel whispered. "Let's go see how well my brilliant plan is working out." She had told him about the costume switch.

"I thought you didn't believe in interfering in romance," Gil teased.

"I don't," Ariel replied with a grin. "I'm just trying to fix Adella's dumb mistakes."

She noticed an otter and a flying fish talking in a corner. "I see Attina and Tedrick," she said to Gil. "Let's go say hi." Ariel figured that by now, Attina, who was pretending to be Adella, should be getting along great with Tedrick. And Adella, who was pretending to be Attina, should be happy with Taz.

"Hi," Ariel said as she swam up to them. "How are you two doing?"

"Fine," Attina said in a not-very-happy voice.

"Good," Ariel said, frowning a little. Attina didn't sound as though she were enjoying herself.

"Hey, who's that under the starfish costume?" a voice from inside the otter costume asked. "Is that Princess Ariel?"

"Yes," Ariel said.

"Nice costume," said the otter. "Although, let's face it, nothing tops my costume. The only way I could look any better," he added with a laugh, "is if I'd come as myself!"

Attina grabbed Ariel's arm and pulled her out of the otter's hearing range. "He's been like that all night," Attina complained through her mask. She shook her head. "I thought

Tedrick was sensitive and intelligent, but it turns out he's just vain and silly. I tried to talk about poetry and literature with him, but all he could talk about was himself or the latest dumb fashion trend. He's just as bad as Taz! And I hate the way he keeps calling me Adella. Maybe I should tell him who I really am so I can end this dumb game and go home."

Ariel shook her head. "No, you can't do that—it would ruin everything!"

Just then a baby seal and a killer whale came rushing by.

"Just leave me alone, Taz!" Adella's voice cried from inside the seal costume. "I can't stand any more Sharkspeare!"

"But Attina," said the boy in the whale costume, "I thought you loved poetry. At least . . . at least that's what my cousin Tedrick told me."

Adella threw up her hands. "Yes, yes, yes, I love poetry. But not all the time! Can't we ever talk about anything fun?"

Attina turned to her date. "And can't *we* ever talk about anything serious?" she demanded.

"All evening long, you just keep asking me how you look," the whale accused Adella. "You're so vain, it's incredible."

"Well, you're so *boring*, it's incredible!" Adella fired back.

"I'm boring? *You're* boring!"

"No, *you're* boring!" The whale waved his flipper wildly and lost his balance, nearly toppling over.

The other princesses noticed the commotion and swam over with their dates.

"I knew this was all a big mistake," the boy in the otter costume complained.

"This is all *your* fault, Ariel," Adella cried. "I should have gone out with Tedrick. He couldn't be any worse than Taz is."

"What do you mean, you *should* have gone out with Tedrick?" the otter demanded.

"I mean I'm not Attina!" Adella ripped off her seal mask and whiskers.

Attina pulled off her own mask. "And I'm not Adella!"

Ariel hung her head. "This is all my fault," she said as everyone fell silent. "See, Adella really liked you, Taz. And Attina really liked you, Tedrick. But everything got all mixed

up, and I tried to unmix it. I told Attina and Adella to switch costumes. It seemed like a foolproof plan."

The otter and the killer whale looked at each other. Suddenly they both burst out laughing.

The otter tossed his mask aside. "I'm not Tedrick," Taz said, still laughing.

Tedrick pulled off his killer whale mask. "And I'm not Taz!"

Taz shook his head with a grin. "See, we both had the same idea. I like Adella, and Tedrick likes Attina, so we switched costumes, too." He gave his cousin an affectionate punch on the arm. "It was all part of Tedrick's brilliant plan."

"It looks as though we had one too many switches!" Ariel cried.

"And one too many brilliant plans," added Andrina, winking at Adella.

"Now that we all know who we really are, maybe we can get on with having a good time," Tedrick said. He blushed as he turned to Attina. "That is, if you'd like to dance with me."

"I'd love to," Attina said shyly.

"Would you like to dance?" Taz asked Adella.

"In a little while," Adella said. "First I need to find a mirror and fix my hair."

"Great idea," Taz agreed. "I'll go fix mine, too."

Ariel shook her head in amazement as she watched the two couples swim away.

"What a mess," Alana said.

"A major mess," Aquata agreed.

"Well, it all worked out for the best," Andrina said. "The important thing is that everybody's happy." She laughed. "But that's the last time I ever try to play matchmaker!"

"Me, too," Alana agreed.

"I think that goes for all of us," Aquata said. "Right, Ariel?"

Ariel didn't answer. She was watching Attina and Tedrick twirl slowly in the middle of the room. Tedrick had his arms wrapped tightly around Attina, who was gazing up into his eyes, a dreamy smile on her face.

"Ariel?" Aquata said a bit louder.

"Hmmm?" Ariel murmured with a distracted sigh. "Don't they look romantic out there?"

Aquata put one arm around her youngest sister's shoulder. "Don't worry, Ariel," she said. "Someday soon I'm sure you'll have someone special to dance with that way."

Ariel smiled. "Thanks, Aquata. I'm sure I will, too. And I'm in no hurry. I know he'll be worth the wait."